This edition published by Parragon Books Ltd in 2016 and distributed by

Parragon Inc.
440 Park Avenue South, 13th Floor
New York, NY 10016
www.parragon.com

Written by Margaret Wise Brown
Illustrated by Marilyn Faucher

ISBN 978-1-4748-6590-6

Printed in China

all the little fathers

PaRragon

Bath • New York • Cologne • Melbourne • Delhi
Hong Kong • Shenzhen • Singapore

All the bear fathers were catching fish with their children.

All the dog fathers were giving their children bones to chew.

All the grasshopper fathers were jumping over their children.

All the squirrel fathers were
hiding nuts for their children.

All the lion fathers were
roaring with their children.

All the monkey fathers

were hanging out with their children.

All the giraffe fathers were helping their children reach up high.

All the bird fathers were bringing
food to their hungry children.

All the horse fathers were

leaping with their children.

All the cat fathers were purring to their children.

All the rabbit fathers were hopping

home with their children.

All the little fathers were putting their children to bed.